ANAKIN TO THE RESCUE!

BY ACE LANDERS   ILLUSTRATED BY DAVID WHITE

SCHOLASTIC INC.

ISBN 978-0-545-47066-7

12 11 10 9 8 7 6 5 4 3 2 1   12 13 14 15 16 17/0

Printed in the U.S.A.   40

First printing, September 2012

OH, DEAR!
ROGER, ROGER!
WOOOSH!
ONLY R2-D2 ESCAPES, THANKS TO HIS BLASTER JETS!

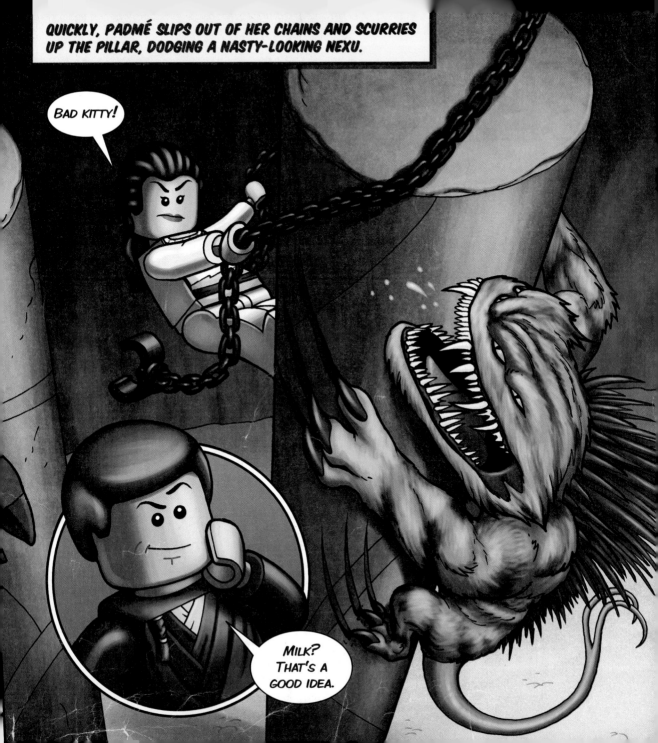